Pearls of Wisdom

Pearls of Wisdom

of

Wisdom

African and Caribbean Folktales

The Listening and Reading Book

Raouf Mama and Mary Romney
Illustrations by Siri Weber Feeney

PRO LINGUA ● ASSOCIATES

Pro Lingua Associates, Publishers

P. O. Box 1348
Brattleboro, Vermont 05302-1348 USA
E-mail: prolingu@sover.net
www.ProLinguaAssociates.com
Office: 802 257 7779
Orders: 800 366 4775
SAN: 216-0579

*At Pro Lingua
our objective is to foster an approach
to learning and teaching that we call
interplay, the **inter**action of language
learners and teachers with their materials,
with the language and culture,
and with each other in active, creative
and productive **play**.*

The stories in this book have been collected from many sources by storyteller Raouf Mama. All but three have been published in two of Dr. Mama's earlier books where he gives a full explanation of his original sources. *How Chameleon Became a Teacher, The Greedy Father, How Yogbo the Glutton Was Tricked,* and *The Prince and the Orphan,* are adapted from stories in *Why Goats Smell Bad and other Stories from Benin* by Raouf Mama. © 1998, Raouf Mama. Reprinted by permission: North Haven, CT: Linnet Books/The Shoe String Press, Inc. *Anancy and the Guinea Bird, How Goat Moved to the Village, Why Cat and Dog Are Always Fighting, A Fisherman and His Dog,* and *Monkey's Argument with Leopard* are adapted from stories in *The Barefoot Book of Tropical Tales,* by Raouf Mama. © 2000, Raouf Mama. Reprinted by permission of Barefoot Books, New York, N.Y. and Bristol, U.K. Raouf Mama's telling of *Pearl of Wisdom, Why Hawk Preys on Chicks* and *The Gold Ring* have not been published before.

This book was designed by Arthur A. Burrows and set in Bookman Oldstyle, a modern, bold adaptation of a traditional square serif face, with Arab Brushstroke, a caligraphic display face; these are both Agfa digital fonts. The book was printed and bound by Boyd Printing Company in Albany, New York.

Printed in the United States of America
First printing 2001. 3000 copies.

Contents

Acknowledgements

So many people have contributed to the making of this book that it is impossible to name all of them. I would like to single out some of them for special thanks, however: Omaa Chukwurah, storyteller, teacher, librarian, and artist, for the gift of the story *Why Hawk Preys on Chicks*; Tessa Strickland and Diantha Thorpe for permission to reprint some of the stories from *Why Goats Smell Bad* and *The Barefoot Book of Tropical Tales;* Lyall and Loretta Powers, Barbara Molette, Sonia Cintron-Marrero, Earna Luering, Christin Jacobi, and my students at Eastern for their encouragement; Eastern Connecticut University and the Connecticut State University system for their support.

Finally, my thanks go forth to my wife, Cherifa, and our children – Faridath, Rabiath, Gemilath, Rahman, and Rahim, for their love, patience, and understanding. *RM*

I wish to thank my husband, Philip Schaab, whose love and support were invaluable in encouraging me during my work on this book. *MR*

Dedications

To Lionel Romney with love,
To Lin and Najid with gratitude,
To the twin boys: Rhaman and Rahim, with thanksgiving.

Raouf Mama

I dedicate this book to my father, Lionel Romney, a wise and wonderful storyteller, and to the memory of my mother, Alice C. Romney, who first inspired my love of stories.

Mary Romney

Introduction

Folktales are one of the oldest forms of literary art, and are to be found in every culture in the world. From the beginning of history, people have used folktales as a traditional means of teaching moral and cultural values and as a tool for educating children and preparing them for adult life. Furthermore, most folktales from one culture have equivalents in another, and this makes them universal. Because of their universality, and the power and simplicity of their language, folktales are ideal for teaching language and literacy skills. This book is an attempt to promote, through the power of folktales, the teaching and learning of English language skills.

All but one of the tales in this book are either from Africa or have African roots. This book contains eight folktales from West Africa, one from Central Africa and three from the Caribbean. Two of the Caribbean stories, in turn, are originally from Africa.

Most of the West African tales are from the Fon ethnic group in the Republic of Benin. The African folktales in this book fall into four broad categories: explanatory tales, sacred tales, trickster tales, and cautionary tales.

Among the Fon tales, *How Chameleon Became a Teacher* is an explanatory tale that describes the origins of the behavior and appearance of chameleons. *The Greedy Father* is a cautionary tale. *The Gold Ring* is a sacred tale. *How Yogbo the Glutton was Tricked* is a trickster tale, and *The Prince and the Orphan* is a sacred tale that is a variant of the Cinderella story.

From the other West African tales, *Why Hawk Preys on Chicks* is an explanatory tale from the Ibo ethnic group, the third largest in Nigeria, whose great oral tradition has yet to be adequately documented. *Why Cat and Dog Are Always Fighting* is also an explanatory tale, this one from Cape Verde, an island nation off the coast of Senegal. *Pearl of Wisdom* is a cautionary tale from Gabon, a French speaking country in West Africa. It came to our attention through a broadcast on "Africa No. 1," a multinational radio station funded by France. The tale is about the importance of names in Gabonese culture in particular, and in African culture in general.

Monkey's Argument with Leopard is a trickster tale from the Democratic Republic of the Congo (formerly Zaire) in Central Africa.

Anancy and the Guinea Bird is a tale from the island of Antigua. Anancy is a character who appears as a trickster in many Caribbean folktales, but who originates from Ghana in West Africa. *How Goat Moved to the Village* is a Haitian tale that calls to mind the biblical story of the un-merciful servant in Matthew 18:23-25. The fact that one of the characters is a hyena and another a lion is an indication of the African origin of the tale. *The Fisherman and His Dog* is a tale from Puerto Rico, where many people of African descent have settled. Taino, the name of the dog, is named after the indigenous people of Puerto Rico.

Two of the Caribbean stories mentioned above are clearly of African origin and, as everyone knows, many people of African descent live not only in the Caribbean but also in North, Central, and South America. This movement of a people from their homeland to other parts of the world is known as a diaspora. *See map on page xiii.*

The African diaspora is the phrase describing the various groups of people of African descent who live outside of Africa. In most cases this diaspora was brought about by the infamous transatlantic slave trade, which took place over three and a half centuries, from the early 16th century through the middle of the 19th century. From 1519 to 1867, approximately 12 million Africans were transported on European slave ships from Africa to the Americas. The slave trade was conducted by trading companies from several European countries: Britain, France, the Netherlands, Spain, Portugal, and Denmark. Thousands of ships carried slaves primarily from the coast of West Africa to many colonies and territories in the Americas.

The forced displacement of people from Africa to the Americas resulted in the transfer of many cultural traditions along with the enslaved people. For example, in the United States, music such as work songs, spirituals, gospel, blues, jazz, and rock and roll have resulted directly from the musical and rhythmic traditions that the slaves brought with them from Africa. In the other countries of the diaspora, different types of music have evolved directly from West African musical traditions.

Another result of the African diaspora has been the spread of the African oral tradition. This oral tradition has survived among people of African descent even into the twenty-first century. This book is a sampling of the multitude of stories from this tradition, collected and told to you by a West African "griot," or storyteller, who brings them to you from his native Africa and countries of the African diaspora.

The African Diaspora

The movement of Africans to the Americas through the slave trade

Where the tales came from:

1. Cape Verde Islands
2. Benin
3. Nigeria
4. Gabon
5. Democratic Republic of the Congo
6. Antigua
7. Puerto Rico
8. Haiti

User's Guide

This collection of stories is also available as **a recording on two cassettes** featuring the voice of Dr. Raouf Mama, the collector of these stories and an established Griot — a masterful West African story teller. The stories on the cassettes follow the stories in this book word-for-word. This book, used with the cassettes, provides valuable practice in listening and reading.

At the end of each story there are some questions called **"Connecting to the Story."** These questions will help you think and talk about the story. By doing this, you can relate these wonderful and wise folktales to your own experiences and life.

The **glossary** will help you understand some of the unusual words in the story. The **Additional Vocabulary** are other useful words that you may or may not know. If you're not sure of them, try to understand the words from the context. First, find the paragraph where the word appears. Then read the sentence with that word to see if you can guess the meaning. Sometimes it is helpful to read the sentences just before and just after the word and its sentence. If you still do not understand the word, look it up in your dictionary. All of the additional vocabulary is also practiced in the workbook that can be used with this book.

The **workbook (Pearls of Wisdom: The Integrated Language Skills Workbook)** contains a variety of activities that provide for work in all skill areas (speaking, listening, reading, writing) and vocabulary development. Each unit of the workbook follows this pattern of activities:

1. Pre-listening
2. Listening
3. Summarizing
4. Vocabulary
5. Reflecting: Writing and Speaking
6. Retelling
7. Concluding

The workbook offers the best way to achieve maximum learning and full enjoyment and appreciation for these stories.

Pearls of Wisdom

African and Caribbean Folktales

How Chameleon Became A Teacher

Benin

Once upon a time, Crocodile and Chameleon were friends. Crocodile was very fond of sunbathing. He loved to come out of the water and to lie on the sand in bright sunshine, and whenever Crocodile came out of the water, Chameleon would come out of the bush and climb up a tree nearby. Soon, they would be talking happily and laughing loudly. Sometimes they would lie very close to each other, whispering, shaking their heads and nodding. They were always deep in thought and discussion. Crocodile and Chameleon were very good friends. *(1)*

One day, Crocodile invited Chameleon to dinner. "Come to my house, at the bottom of the lake," he said, "and my family will give you a delicious meal. We'll have fun together afterwards. When you see me rise to the surface, jump into the lake and I will take you to my house." They agreed on a day and a time, Chameleon thanked Crocodile for his kindness, and they said goodbye to each other. *(2)*

On the day they had agreed to meet, Chameleon went to the shore of the lake, carrying a stick. While Chameleon waited, Crocodile gathered his wife and children together in their house at the bottom of the lake. He said, "Rejoice! Rejoice! My friend Chameleon is coming to see us! He will be our special meal! I cannot tell you what a delicacy he will be! Chameleon meat is so tasty." *(3)*

Crocodile then went out to meet his friend. There was a great splashing on the surface of the lake as he came to the shore. His gigantic mouth was wide open. To test his friend, Chameleon threw his stick into the water. Believing that Chameleon had dived into the lake, Crocodile rushed forward and closed his enormous mouth over the stick. *(4)*

1

Chameleon was shaking, trembling in terror. His heart was racing furiously. Chameleon fled from the shore and quickly climbed the closest tree. Then, blending in with the color of the leaves, he cried, "What would have happened to me if I had not thrown my stick into the lake to test my friend! Thank Goodness I did not jump into the lake to meet Crocodile. I would have ended up in the bottom of his stomach instead of as a guest at his house at the bottom of the lake. Take note! Take note, oh world! Caution is the mother of safety!" *(5)*

And so it was that Chameleon became a teacher of prudence and wisdom. He walks very slowly and carefully, he thinks long and hard before putting a foot forward, and he takes on the local color wherever he happens to be. *(6)*

How Chameleon Became A Teacher

Connecting to the story

Think about and discuss these questions:

Do you believe it is wise to blend in and take on the local color in a new environment? Why?

Have you ever had an experience like Chameleon's experience with Crocodile? Explain.

Glossary

(Numbers refer to the paragraph number)

Words

the bush (1), n. — land where people do not live

rejoice (3), v. — be happy

tasty (3), adj. — delicious

prudence (6), n. — carefulness, thinking before acting

Phrasal verbs and verb-preposition combinations

blending in (5) — becoming the same, mixing together

ended up (5) — finished, completed, came to a final result

Additional Vocabulary

Do you know these words and phrases?

____ to be fond of (1)   ____ enormous (4)

____ to nod (1)   ____ to tremble (5)

____ delicacy, delicious (3)   ____ to flee, fled (5)

____ to splash (4)   ____ guest (5)

____ gigantic (4)   ____ wisdom, wise (6)

Look them up or look for them in the workbook.

Why Hawk Preys on Chicks

Nigeria

Long ago, when the earth was new, the birds of the air and the animals of the field were friends. Hawk was the only exception, for Hawk was always preying on small, weak animals and their young. One day, the animals of the field sent a messenger to Hawk. *(1)*

"Go tell him to stop hunting and killing us," the animals of the field told the messenger. And Hawk replied, "I will gladly stop hunting and killing if you will choose one of you to hunt and kill so I can feed myself and my little ones." *(2)*

Hawk's request put the animals in great difficulty, for they did not know who to offer as a sacrifice. There were no volunteers of course, for no one wanted to be food for Hawk. Finally, the animals decided to hold a meeting to discuss the matter. *(3)*

On the day of the meeting, as all the animals in the village were arriving at the public arena where the meeting was going to be held, Chicken was seen going in the opposite direction. *(4)*

"Where are you going?" the animals asked Chicken. "Have you forgotten our meeting today?" *(5)*

"Not at all," Chicken replied, smoothing her feathers. "There is something else I must do today." Now, Chicken had a habit of not attending meetings and that day was no exception. "Listen," Chicken continued, "I am sure that you are capable of making wise decisions. I will have no problem with whatever decision you make, none at all."
And with a self-satisfied shake of the head, Chicken strutted off on her way, leaving the animals staring after her. *(6)*

5

Soon afterwards, all the animals gathered in the arena to decide who should be offered to Hawk as a sacrificial victim. There was much squabbling and no agreement in sight. *(7)*

Then one of the animals who had spoken to Chicken said, "Why are we arguing? Why are we wasting our time? Didn't Chicken say that she would have no problem with any decision we make?" All the animals nodded in agreement. "Well then, let's offer Chicken to Hawk as a sacrifice!" *(8)*

Shouts of joy and relief filled the air as the animals jumped up and down, congratulating each other on the outcome of their meeting. *(9)*

A messenger was immediately sent to Hawk who promptly agreed to the decision. And that is why, to this day, Hawk preys on Chicken and her chicks. *(10)*

Why Hawk Preys on Chicks

Connecting to the story

Think about and discuss these questions:

Do you think some animals should be protected and others sacrificed? Why?

What is your opinion about hunting?

Is it fair for people to hunt animals as a sport?

Glossary

(Numbers refer to the paragraph number)

Words

young (1), n — baby animals

smoothing (6), v. — making a surface flat and neat

strutted (6), v. — walked in a proud way

Phrasal verbs and verb-preposition combinations

preys on (title, 10) — hunts, kills, and eats

Additional Vocabulary

Do you know these words and phrases?

____ sacrifice, sacrificial (3, 7)   ____ to squabble (7)

____ arena (4)   ____ promptly (10)

____ victim (7)

Look them up or look for them in the workbook.

Pearl of Wisdom

Gabon

Long ago, there lived a powerful king. And because he was powerful, he thought he was also the strongest, the wealthiest, the most handsome, and the wisest human being that had ever walked the earth. But he was a tyrant. *(1)*

Under his reign no newborn child could have any name except the one chosen by the king. And so mean was the king that he always chose bad, insulting names: Pig-Head, Dirty, Slob, Ugly, Smelly, Fatty, Bad Breath, Alligator-Skin, etc... These were the kinds of names the king gave babies born in his kingdom. No one really liked the names, but everyone pretended they were just perfect because they were afraid of the king. *(2)*

One day a woman gave birth to a beautiful baby boy; but instead of letting the king give him a name, she decided to name the child herself. "I shall call you Pearl of Wisdom," she whispered softly into his ears, "for I value wisdom above all gifts. May you live to be wise like your name." *(3)*

Never had a mother chosen a more perfect name for her son, for Pearl of Wisdom grew into an exceedingly wise little boy. He was only seven years old when he won a riddle-solving contest organized by the king to test his people. *(4)*

"What eats and eats and is never satisfied?"

"What runs and runs and is never tired?"

"What comes riding a swift horse and goes back dragging its feet?" *(5)*

No one had an answer to these riddles, no one except Pearl of Wisdom. *(6)*

"Fire eats and eats and is never satisfied. The river runs and runs and is never tired. Disease comes riding a swift horse and goes back dragging its feet." *(7)*

The king and all his advisors were amazed. "What is your name?" the king asked the little boy, trying to find out more about him. And when he said that his name was Pearl of Wisdom, a shadow passed over the king's face. *(8)*

"I see," the king said, struggling to hide the anger rising in him. "You are very wise indeed, but whoever gave you that name has done it behind my back! That person has broken the law of the land and must face the consequences!" *(9)*

In no time at all, the mother was brought before the king "So, you have ignored the law of the land and named your child behind my back!" the king growled, his eyes as red as fire. "You have named your child Pearl of Wisdom! For this, you should be put to death. But I am a merciful king, so I will spare your life if you can show me that you know more than I do." *(10)*

So speaking, the king handed to her grains of corn and said, "I am entertaining guests tomorrow and I need a lot of beer. Plant these grains, harvest them and make beer out of them by sunrise tomorrow, and I will leave you alone. But if you fail to accomplish the task, you will lose your life." *(11)*

The woman fell to her knees, weeping and begging the king to have mercy, but it was all in vain. The king would not go back on his word. She would either have to carry out the task or pay for it with her life. *(12)*

As soon as they got home, Pearl of Wisdom and his mother whispered together a long time. Then, the mother hurried out of the house and went straight to the palace, clutching in her right hand something her son had given her. *(13)*

At the palace she requested an urgent meeting with the king and her request was granted. And kneeling down before the king, the mother opened her right hand, where the king saw some seeds. *(14)*

"These, your Royal Highness, are calabash seeds. If you will plant them and harvest them before sunrise tomorrow, I will have calabashes into which I will pour beer for the guests at your feast." *(15)*

"You are asking me to perform an impossible task," the king said. "How can I grow and harvest calabashes before sunrise tomorrow?" *(16)*

"Your Royal Highness is right," the mother said, smiling gently. "You cannot grow and harvest calabash before sunrise tomorrow, nor can I plant corn, harvest it and make beer out of it in a day." *(17)*

That very night, the king appointed Pearl of Wisdom and his mother to the royal council, and the next day a royal proclamation was issued to allow people to name their children freely. And so it has been to this day. *(18)*

Pearl of Wisdom

Connecting to the story

Think about and discuss these questions:

How do people decide on names of their children in your country / culture?

Have you ever lived in a country with a king, queen, or emperor?

What do you think should be the role of the king or queen of a country?

Glossary

(Numbers refer to the paragraph number)

Words and Phrases

riddle (4), n. — a puzzle, usually a question

consequences (9), n. — the results of an action

calabash (15), n.
— a vegetable like a squash that can be used for a pot

Your Royal Highness (15), n.
— the phrase that is used when talking to a king or queen

proclamation (18), n. — an official announcement

Phrasal verbs and verb-preposition combinations

find out (8) — discover, learn

carry out (12) — do something; follow instructions

Additional Vocabulary

Do you know these words and phrases?

____ tyrant (1)   ____ merciful, mercy (10,12)

____ reign (2)   ____ to harvest (11)

____ mean (2)   ____ task (11)

____ to pretend (2)   ____ weep (12)

____ exceedingly (4)   ____ to clutch (13)

____ to ignore (10)   ____ seed (14)

Look them up or look for them in the workbook.

Anancy
and the Guinea Bird

Antigua

Hard times had come to the land. A terrible drought had burned the grass and the trees. The drought had dried the big river that gave the village all its water. No one could remember a drought like this. Anancy, the spider, was hungry and had no food. He knew he must find a way to fill his stomach, or die a terrible death. What could he do? Anancy thought long and hard, but he could find no answer. Then an idea came to him; he decided to get Father God to make a new law. *(1)*

"The world would be a better place if people did not interfere in the lives of their neighbors," Anancy told Father God. "Make a new law: anyone who does not mind their own business must die. Let them just drop down dead." Father God considered Anancy's words and they pleased him. He accepted Anancy's recommendation and made the new law. *(2)*

Happy with this new law, Anancy immediately started to make a garden on the rocks of the mountainside. He got out his garden tools – a hoe, a machete and a pickaxe – and he started to chip away at the rock. He was pretending to cultivate his garden. *(3)*

Soon Goat came walking past Anancy's garden. "What is Anancy doing?" he asked in surprise and confusion. "Trying to grow food on rocks?" But the moment he asked the question, he dropped dead on the spot where he spoke. *(4)*

Quickly, Anancy took Goat to his house and made a good meal of him. It was the first time Anancy had eaten in a very long while. *(5)*

"Well," he said, rubbing his big belly and belching noisily, "wherever you are, I hope you have learned a lesson, stupid Goat. Think twice before interfering in other people's lives!" *(6)*

The next day Anancy returned to his garden and once again made a big show of chipping away at the rock. Soon Pig came by, and he too was amazed to see Anancy striking at the rock with his pickaxe. *(7)*

"Anancy!" he grunted. "Trying to grow food from stone! Surely you know better than that!" And like Goat before him, Pig dropped down dead on the spot where he spoke. *(8)*

As the days went by many, many more animals suffered the same destiny: Buffalo, Lion, Vulture, Elephant, Parrot, Hyena. Anancy caught them all in his fatal trap. They all fell for Anancy's deadly trick and ended up in his stomach. *(9)*

Everyone was dying of hunger, except Anancy. So while the whole land was starving, Anancy grew fat, for he had an endless supply of meat in his house. And he would have eaten all the birds and animals if Guinea Bird had not spied on Anancy and decided to turn his own trickery against him. *(10)*

Now, Guinea Bird was almost completely bald with just a few feathers on the top of his head. He found a horse and saddle and made a song which he practiced for weeks in preparation for his encounter with Anancy. *(11)*

And so it was that one morning, while Anancy was chipping away at the rock in his garden, Guinea Bird came riding past on his horse. He was singing loudly: "All boys who go to the barber shop comb their hair like me!" *(12)*

Guinea Bird rode past Anancy in one direction, then turned around and rode past him again in the other direction. And as he rode up and down, he kept turning his bald head and singing: "All boys who go to the barber shop comb their hair like me!" *(13)*

Anancy was speechless. "This is ridiculous! What kind of nonsense is this?" he cried, as he watched Guinea Bird majestically riding his horse, turning his bald head from side to side, and passing his hand over it proudly. Struggling to keep his self-control, Anancy went on chipping away at the rock in his garden. But Guinea Bird kept riding up and down the path by Anancy's garden, singing all the time. *(14)*

Anancy found it increasingly difficult to go on working. But he did his best to ignore Guinea Bird and his silly song. Finally he stopped working and, leaning on his pickaxe, simply watched Guinea Bird for the rest of the morning, hoping he would lose his voice and leave him alone. *(15)*

But Guinea Bird went on singing as loudly as ever. What was Anancy going to do? He tried not to lose patience. But that was hard, like not scratching an itching spot. Anancy tried to stop himself from speaking, and when that didn't work he bit his tongue, and when that didn't work he closed his eyes, hoping that Guinea Bird would go away and his song fade into silence. But it was all in vain. *(16)*

Finally Anancy looked up to the heavens and said, "Father God, I got you to make this law, but I must ask you: what does Guinea Bird have on his head to comb?" *(17)*

And the moment he spoke those words, Anancy dropped down dead. *(18)*

Anancy and the Guinea Bird

Connecting to the story

Think about and discuss these questions:

Have you ever experienced a natural disaster like the drought in this story?

Do you think it's best to mind your own business or to ask what your neighbors are doing?

Glossary

(Numbers refer to the paragraph number)

Words

drought (1), n. — a long period of time with no rain

interfere (2), v.
— to come uninvited between someone and their work; to get in the way

belching (6), v.
— letting air out of the stomach through the mouth making a noise

destiny (9), n. — final outcome or result; fate

Phrasal verbs and verb-preposition combinations

fell for (9) — were tricked by, fooled by, out smarted by

spied on (10) — were watched secretly

Additional Vocabulary

Do you know these words and phrases?

____ to chip away (3)   ____ bald (11)

____ to grunt (8)   ____ majestically (14)

____ fatal (9)   ____ to ignore (15)

____ trickery (10)   ____ to fade (16)

Look them up or look for them in the workbook.

How Goat Moved to the Village

Haiti

One afternoon, Goat was sitting by a fire just outside his house in the jungle, baking sweet potatoes. He had worked very hard during the planting season so he had a good harvest. Now he was going to satisfy his hunger for fresh-baked sweet potatoes. *(1)*

He blew on the ashes and stirred the fire, and soon the delicious smell of sweet potatoes went floating through the jungle, carried along by the breeze. When the fire burned itself out, Goat, licking his lips, got a stick and quickly took out the big, steaming sweet potatoes from under the ashes. Grabbing a sweet potato, he blew on it: "Pff . . . pff . . . pff . . ." *(2)*

But before he could bite into it, a voice called out behind him: "Good afternoon." *(3)*

Goat jumped up and dropped the sweet potato, as if those words had turned the potato into a red-hot coal. When he turned around, he saw Hyena standing in back of him. Hyena's eyes were shining with bad intentions. "Good afternoon," Goat replied. His voice was trembling in fear. "You have arrived just in time for a meal. Come and help yourself to fresh-baked sweet potatoes." *(4)*

"I'm starving," Hyena replied, looking hungrily at Goat, "but I will eat no sweet potatoes." *(5)*

"I have cassava and sweet corn, if you can wait a few moments," Goat said, struggling to hide his fear. *(6)*

"I am really hungry," Hyena answered, "but I am not hungry for cassava or sweet corn. I am hungry for you!" *(7)*

Shivers ran down Goat's back. He wanted to run away, but where could he run? He knew Hyena could always catch up with him. *(8)*

"My grandfather and yours were great friends. They were so close . . . ," Goat said, trying to talk his way out of danger. *(9)*

"Shut up!" Hyena screamed, clawing the air in anger. "What do I care about your grandfather! I am hungry, not for words or friendship, but for goat-meat!" *(10)*

Seeing that Hyena wanted to eat, not talk, Goat quickly changed his strategy. He took a sweet potato and made a great show of biting into it. The sweet potato tasted like ashes, but that didn't prevent Goat from smacking his lips. He took little bites, but he chewed on and on. Goat was buying time while looking to escape from the jaws of death. Despite his hunger, Hyena decided to wait a little while. Hyena wanted Goat to eat as much as possible so that Goat would be big enough to fill his stomach. As Goat ate on and on, however, Hyena's patience ran out. "What is taking you so long?" he howled. "I cannot wait here all evening while you go on eating. That bite will be your last one. I am starving!" *(11)*

He came toward Goat, his eyes shining, his claws itching to get at him. *(12)*

At that moment, they heard a loud, blood-chilling noise that sounded like thunder as Lion came walking toward them. *(13)*

"Good afternoon," Lion roared, glaring at both Hyena and Goat. "Good afternoon," Hyena stammered, but Goat remained silent. *(14)*

"You look so sad, as if you had been sentenced to death. What's the matter with you?" Lion said, fixing his eyes on Goat with a fierce gaze. *(15)*

"I was about to eat my fresh-baked sweet potatoes when Hyena came by. I invited him to join in. I offered to cook cassava and sweet corn for him if he preferred, but he said he was going to eat me instead. I don't think he's being fair. Maybe you can settle the matter." *(16)*

"I really cannot say whether Hyena is fair or unfair," Lion replied, staring at Hyena with hunger in his eyes. "But it seems to me there is only one way to settle such a delicate matter. Let Goat eat his sweet potatoes, let Hyena eat Goat, so I can eat Hyena! That will settle the matter once and for all!" Hyena felt numb all over and broke out in a sweat. He thought Lion's solution was terribly unfair, but he was silenced by the look in the big cat's eyes. *(17)*

Trying to put a good face on a disaster, Hyena laid his paw on Goat's neck, and shaking him said. "Hurry up and finish your sweet potatoes, so I can eat you up, and Lion can eat me. But first I must step into the bush to relieve myself. Excuse me a moment." And Hyena disappeared into the bush. *(18)*

A few moments later, Goat saw Hyena running as fast as he could. He was running for his life. "Your food is running away," Goat shouted to Lion, pointing in the direction Hyena was running. In a flash, Lion went flying through the jungle in hot pursuit of Hyena. *(19)*

Goat sprang to his feet and ran in the opposite direction. Promising never to return to the jungle, Goat ran straight to the village. Soon afterwards, his parents and all his relatives joined him. But whether Goat and his family intended to remain in the village or live somewhere else is still a mystery. *(20)*

How Goat Moved from the Jungle to the Village

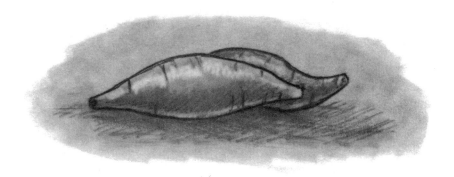

Connecting to the story

Think about and discuss these questions:

Have you ever moved from a rural area to an urban one?
Why?

Have you ever been in a dangerous situation that you
escaped from? Explain.

Glossary

(Numbers refer to the paragraph number)

Words

cassava (16), n. — A root vegetable, somewhat like a potato.

Phrasal verbs and verb-preposition combinations

turned into (4) — changed; became something else

catch up with (8)
— come from behind to the same place as someone else

talk (someone) out of (9)
— convince someone not to do something

ran out (11) — finished; consumed completely

came by (16) — visited, stopped to visit

broke out in a sweat(17) — suddenly started to sweat

Additional Vocabulary

Do you know these words and phrases?

_____ harvest (1)	_____ to chew (11)
_____ ashes (2)	_____ to howl (11)
_____ to bite (3)	_____ fierce (15)
_____ to struggle (6)	_____ numb (17)
_____ to claw (10)	

Look them up or look for them in the workbook.

The Greedy Father

Benin

Once upon a time in a small village, there lived a man named Nadjo. He was very poor and lived in a crumbling shack. But he had a beautiful daughter named Gbessi. She was tall, with big, bright eyes and a wonderful smile. Nadjo could hardly wait until she was old enough to get married. When he looked at her, he could only think about the bags of gold her beauty would bring him as a bride-price. *(1)*

All the young men in the village were fascinated by Gbessi's beauty and they all wanted to marry her. Countless handsome men came forward and asked for her hand in marriage. They were strong, hard-working men. Some of them brought half the provisions in their barns, and rolls of fine fabrics. But Nadjo was not satisfied. *(2)*

Other men brought all the provisions in their barns, rolls of fine fabrics, and jewelry. Still Gbessi's father was not satisfied. None of the young men was rich enough to pay the bride-price he wanted. Gbessi was an obedient daughter, so she turned down all the marriage proposals from the men of the village. One after another, the young men went away broken-hearted. *(3)*

One day, a monkey living in the jungle heard about Gbessi's great beauty and her father's enormous greed. He was a very ugly monkey, but he was very smart. He decided he was going to marry the beautiful Gbessi. He made himself beautiful clothes from the fabrics he had stolen. Ant built him a beautiful house. Dog, Lion, and Panther supplied him with plenty of meat. Elephant offered him firewood, Bee brought him honey, Hare brought him yams and cassava, and Partridge brought him millet and corn. Eagle gave him expensive necklaces and bangles, and Squirrel brought him gold and diamonds. *(4)*

The generosity of Monkey's friends made him very wealthy, and with his own magical powers he transformed

27

himself into a handsome man. And so it was that Monkey set out for Gbessi's village, carrying expensive gifts and dressed up as a wealthy, handsome young man. *(5)*

Monkey arrived with gorgeous fabrics, priceless jewels, and loads of provisions. The moment Nadjo saw Monkey, his clothes and the gifts he had brought, Nadjo was convinced he had found the ideal husband for his daughter. And Gbessi found Monkey more handsome than all the men who had proposed to her and she wanted to marry only him. *(6)*

"I can see that you will make a wonderful husband for my daughter," Nadjo said, fingering the diamonds, the gold and the jewels Monkey had displayed in front of him. "But you cannot marry my daughter unless you bring more provisions and bags of gold and diamonds." *(7)*

Monkey was amazed at Nadjo's greed, but he quickly recovered and said, "What I am offering you is only a token of my love, for your daughter is priceless. If you let me take your beautiful daughter with me, I will make you the happiest man on earth before the year is over." Nadjo had no reason to doubt Monkey's promise, and he gave his permission immediately. *(8)*

The wedding was unbelievable. People came from far and near in their best and most expensive clothes, but no one was more beautifully dressed than Gbessi and her groom. Food and drink were plentiful. There was palm wine, and beer, rice and chicken, beef stew, yam, bush meat soup, black-eyed peas with palm oil and red corn paste. And there was much dancing and singing. Monkey showered singers and dancers with gold coins. *(9)*

At the end of the wedding ceremony, Gbessi set out for her new home with her handsome young husband. Every morning thereafter, Monkey and his wife worked on the new farm he had bought. And for a few months they lived happily, working the land as farmers. *(10)*

Monkey soon got tired of his new life, however. He found the clothing of men to be more and more uncomfortable. And the interminable days of hard work on the farm were boring and tiring. His monkey nature could not endure this tiresome, monotonous life. He missed the company of the other monkeys. He missed swinging from one tree to another. He missed running, playing, climbing and chattering all day long or stealing food from farms and running off at the first sign of danger. *(11)*

Then, one day, while Monkey and Gbessi were working the land in preparation for the planting season, Monkey threw down his hoe in disgust and frustration. Moving away from his wife, he said a few magical words. Suddenly he turned back into a monkey! Gbessi heard her husband say something, and when she turned to ask what he had said, she was shocked to see a hideous monkey instead of her husband. He was taking off his man-made clothes. His tail was still missing, but Gbessi watched in total amazement as it grew back. *(12)*

She was paralyzed with horror. Then she realized that she had married a hideous monkey. She cried out in fear and began to run. Monkey ran behind her in hot pursuit, driven by anger and fear of being discovered. *(13)*

Gbessi was a fast runner, and she ran swiftly through the jungle. She leaped over fallen tree trunks, wide holes and ditches, streams and boulders. But Monkey gained on her steadily. He knew the jungle and all the shortcuts through its thickets. *(14)*

Soon Gbessi could feel Monkey's hot breath on her back. At that moment, however, she saw her village in the distance, and she knew that safety was near. She increased her speed and put a few meters between herself and Monkey. She ran through the gate to her father's compound crying, "Father, help me! Father, save me!" Nadjo rushed out of the house upon hearing his daughter's cry for help. But Monkey made a giant leap forward and touched her on the shoulder. Nadjo saw his beautiful Gbessi turned into a monkey right in front of his eyes. Her hair turned coarse and stiff and spread all over her body. Her graceful arms and legs withered. Her monkey face grimaced as she turned away from her heartbroken father to her new home in the jungle. *(15)*

Within days, Nadjo went insane with sadness and the guilt of his own greed. He died soon thereafter. *(16)*

The Greedy Father

Connecting to the story

Think about and discuss these questions:

How important is material wealth in determining happiness?

In your country / culture what is the role of parents in the marriage of their children?

If you are not living in your country, do you think marriage is different in your country from the country where you are now living?

Glossary

(Numbers refer to the paragraph number)

Words

palm wine (9), n. — an alcoholic drink made from palm nuts

yam (9), n. — a large root vegetable, somewhat like a potato

bush meat soup (9), n.
— a West African soup made with beef

black-eyed peas with palm oil (9), n.
— beans and the oil from palm nuts

red corn paste (9), n. — a thick sauce

hoe (12), n.
— a farming tool with a metal blade at the end of a long handle

leaped (14), v. — jumped over something

boulders (14), n. — large rocks

thickets (14), n. — many bushes growing close together

Phrasal verbs and verb-preposition combinations

came forward (2) — offered or presented oneself

turned down (3) — rejected an offer

set out for (5) — began a trip

taking off (12) — removing clothes

gained on (14) — got closer to

Additional Vocabulary

Do you know these words and phrases?

_____ greed(y) (title, 4)   _____ to chatter (11)

_____ to crumble (1)   _____ to realize (13)

_____ bride-price (1)   _____ hideous (13)

_____ countless (2)   _____ to drive (13)

_____ provisions (2)   _____ swiftly (14)

_____ obedient (3)   _____ thicket (14)

_____ fabric (4)   _____ compound (15)

_____ token (8)   _____ to wither (15)

_____ to endure (11)   _____ heartbroken (15)

                                              _____ insane (16)

Look them up or look for them in the workbook.

Why Cat and Dog are Always Fighting

Cape Verde

Long ago, when the world was new, Cat and Dog were friends. In the village where Cat and Dog lived, no friendship had ever lasted so long. No friendship had ever caused so much envy or so much admiration. Cat and Dog gathered food together, they ate together, and they stored their provisions together. Wherever one went, the other went, too. They watched out for each other. They took care of each other. It seemed that nothing could cause problems between the two friends. They were like brothers. *(1)*

But suddenly one season, their village was struck by a terrible famine. It was almost impossible for Cat and Dog to find food. One day they couldn't find anything to eat. They searched and searched, but they found no food. *(2)*

"What are we going to do?" Cat mewed. *(3)*

"I don't know," Dog whimpered, "but we must go on searching for food." *(4)*

Cat and Dog continued searching. Suddenly they smelled the delicious aroma of fresh cheese. The aroma came floating to them on the evening air. It tickled their noses, and made their stomachs burn with hunger. The two friends lifted their heads and sniffed hungrily. They looked around the village. Soon Cat and Dog came to a small house. Smoke was rising and drifting over the roof. Cat and Dog whispered together. Then, they separated and positioned themselves at the front and back of the house. Cat was near the entrance, while Dog was at the back. Dog started barking and yelping wildly. He was jumping up and down, as if he was trying to warn the owners of the house of some danger. *(5)*

Soon a man and a woman came out of the house and ran around to the back. There, they saw a strange dog. They stared at Dog, trying to understand the reason for his alarm. While they were looking at Dog, Cat dashed into the house and took off with a large piece of fresh cheese. *(6)*

Then Dog ran away from the house. When he found his friend, Cat, they discussed how to divide the cheese; but they could not agree. "To make sure each of us gets an equal part of the cheese, let's call on Donkey to help us divide it," Dog panted. "He is an animal of few words, but he is fair-minded." *(7)*

"Fair-minded?" Cat replied. "He is so stupid he can't even think! A donkey cannot help to settle an argument! I prefer to call on Goat. He is honest, and his beard is a sign of his intelligence." *(8)*

"Don't be silly!" Dog growled. "That stinking Goat will make the food smell bad. He will ruin my appetite!" *(9)*

Cat and Dog argued and argued. They could not agree. Whatever one offered, the other rejected. After Cat and Dog had argued for a long time, Monkey's name came up. Cat and Dog quickly agreed that Monkey would be the best one to settle the argument and divide the cheese. So they hurried to Monkey's house. *(10)*

When Cat and Dog arrived at Monkey's house, he greeted them, "I'm glad to see you, my friends. What brings you to my house? It has been a long time . . . ," but he stopped in the middle of his sentence when he saw the cheese. He licked his lips with hunger and greed. *(11)*

"We need to know how to divide the cheese equally," Cat and Dog shouted, holding the stolen food for Monkey to see. "Only you can help us." *(12)*

"With pleasure," Monkey replied, smiling falsely. "This is something I do every day. I do it for strangers, so I will certainly do it for my friends." Monkey got a knife and scales. But instead of cutting the cheese into two equal parts, he made one piece larger than the other. *(13)*

"This isn't right," Monkey cried. He shook his head as he weighed the two pieces of cheese on the scale. "This isn't right at all!" Quickly he bit off part of the heavier piece and ate it. Cat and Dog were shocked as they watched Monkey. But Monkey had bitten off so much that the heavier piece was now the lighter piece. "What have I done?" Monkey moaned, holding his head in his hands. "Am I crazy?" To make the two parts equal, he bit off some of the other piece. *(14)*

Cat and Dog saw that half the cheese they had brought to Monkey was now gone. They jumped up and demanded, "Give us the rest of the cheese so that we can divide it between ourselves." *(15)*

"No," said Monkey, as he continued greedily eating the cheese. "I hate to do things by halves. I must protect my reputation for wisdom. And I must preserve the friendship between the two of you." *(16)*

Cat and Dog leaped at Monkey, but he quickly escaped. Carrying the rest of the cheese in one hand, Monkey scrambled up a tree and disappeared. Cat and Dog then turned on each other. Their eyes were burning with anger, and their teeth were flashing. "You must pay for this! Monkey was your choice!" Cat screeched. *(17)*

"Not me! You said Monkey was a good judge," Dog howled. And Cat and Dog started fighting, scratching, biting, arguing, screaming, and hissing. *(18)*

From then until now, Cat and Dog have been angry at each other. Even when they seem to have made peace, the old argument is still there, just below the surface, and it can suddenly burst into flame any time Cat and Dog are together. *(19)*

Why Cat and Dog are Always Fighting

Connecting to the story

Think about and discuss these questions:

Have you ever been in a serious disagreement with anyone? What was the cause?

Does the constant fight between cat and dog remind you of any other conflicts?

Has anything ever been stolen from you? What was the result?

Glossary

(Numbers refer to the paragraph number)

Words

envy (1), n. — wanting something others have (also: to envy)

admiration (1), n.
— great respect for someone or something (also: to admire)

dashed (6), v. — ran a short way very quickly

Phrasal verbs and verb-preposition combinations

watch out for (1) — protect; guard

go on (4) — continue

take off with (6) — steal and escape with something

call on (7) — ask for help

came up (10) — was mentioned

Additional Vocabulary

Do you know these words and phrases?

____ famine (2)	____ to lick (11)
____ to search (2)	____ scales (13)
____ aroma (5)	____ reputation (16)
____ to sniff (5)	____ wisdom (16)
____ to yelp (5)	____ to screech (16)
____ to pant (7)	____ to howl (18)
____ to growl (9)	____ to scream (18)
____ to argue (10)	____ to hiss (18)

Look them up or look for them in the workbook.

A Fisherman
and His Dog

Puerto Rico

Once there lived an old fisherman in San Juan. Don Manolito was his name. He was tall and thin, with a headful of greying, silver hair. He had a sad, childlike smile. Don Manolito lived in a little hut at the edge of town. No one really knew how he came to settle in San Juan. Some people said he had come from a remote part of Puerto Rico, sorrowful and broken-hearted after the death of his beloved wife. *(1)*

Don Manolito was a man of few words. He was kind and friendly, but he had no close friend except for his dog, Taino. Taino was a quiet, gentle creature with shining black hair and long, pointed ears. Whether Don Manolito was going to the market place or walking around town, Taino always accompanied him, running or walking by his side, with his ears perked up, his tongue hanging out. Whenever a visitor came to Don Manolito's hut, Taino would sit at Don Manolito's feet, a silent listener to the conversation. *(2)*

Don Manolito usually went fishing several days a week, and he never set sail without Taino walking with him to the edge of the sea. There, Taino would remain until Don Manolito came rowing his boat back in the evening. *(3)*

Don Manolito always saved the best fish for their evening meal. Soon after they returned home, the delicious smell of food filled the air. And anyone who came through their door at that moment was sure to get a warm welcome and a good meal. To the people of San Juan, the sight of Don Manolito and Taino setting out for the seashore in the morning and coming back in the evening, and the delicious smell of food which followed their return became a ritual, a part of the natural rhythm of life. It was like the ebb and flow of the ocean, sunrise and sunset, the waxing and waning of the moon. *(4)*

One morning, soon after Don Manolito's boat had vanished from sight, the sky gradually covered itself with dark clouds. As the sun grew dimmer and dimmer and the wind gathered strength, the silence was broken now and then by the rumbling of distant thunder. People ran in every direction to finish their errands before returning to the protection of their homes. Fishermen came rowing furiously ashore, bringing tales of a storm raging fiercely at sea. *(5)*

In no time at all the seashore was empty, except for Taino. As the thunder rumbled louder, and the sky grew darker, Taino sat patiently and looked out to sea, waiting for Don Manolito to come rowing his boat ashore. But there was neither sight nor sound of Don Manolito or his rowboat. *(6)*

While Taino was waiting, the storm burst over the town with flashes of lightning and explosions of thunder. And the sea roared in response, sending towering waves crashing upon the shore. Taino was swept off his feet again and again as the waves rushed upon him. Finally he threw himself into the sea and swam all the way to a rock jutting out of the roaring waters. The storm raged all evening and far into the night. *(7)*

Taino kept his vigil, high on the rock jutting out of the stormy water. Hour after hour, he sat there, looking out to sea and waiting for Don Manolito to come rowing his boat ashore. But there was neither sight nor sound of Don Manolito or his rowboat. *(8)*

As night slowly brightened into dawn, the storm gradually ended and the roll of thunder grew more and more distant until it was silent. The ferocious sea was silenced and everywhere in San Juan life went back to normal. Yet high on the rock above the waters, Taino remained sitting, looking out to sea and waiting for Don Manolito to come rowing his boat ashore. But there was neither sight nor sound of Don Manolito or his rowboat. *(9)*

Suddenly someone pointed at the rock and a shout went up, followed by another and another. Soon, from one end of the shore to the other, exclamations of amazement rose to the heavens. Quickly the fishermen jumped into their boats and rowed as fast as they could towards the rock. "It's Taino!" cried a fisherman who had rowed ahead of the rest. And soon all were shouting; "It's Taino! It's Taino!" But why and how Taino came to be on that rock was a mystery none could understand. *(10)*

Then they realized that Don Manolito had not been seen since rowing out to sea the day before and that Taino had been sitting on that rock through the storm and through the night, waiting for his friend. A chill ran down their spines and they all fell silent, for they knew then that Don Manolito had been caught up in the terrible storm and would never come back. *(11)*

"Let's take Taino back to shore, for he must be cold and hungry," said one of the fishermen as he climbed onto the rock. But when he laid his hands on the dog to pick him up, he cried out in dismay. Taino had turned to stone! The sad news of Taino's transformation spread through San Juan and the whole island. *(12)*

The people who knew Taino and Don Manolito in person and who lived through those fearful days have long gone out of this world. Memory of the storm which overwhelmed Don Manolito at sea is lost in the mists of time. San Juan has grown into a bustling metropolis. But on a rock off the coast of the modern city, a dog of stone still sits, looking out to sea in silent testimony to the greatest friendship ever to unite a fisherman and his dog. *(13)*

A Fisherman and His Dog

Connecting to the story

Think about and discuss these questions:

Do you think dogs are the best pets? Why?

What are the most important characteristics of a good friend?

Glossary

(Numbers refer to the paragraph number)

Words and phrases

set sail (3), v. — bagin a trip by sailboat, putting up the sail

waxing and waning of the moon (4), n. — the change in the moon over a month from the dark of the moon to the full (round) moon and back to the dark of the moon (wax = grow, increase; wane = shrink, decrease)

ebb and flow (4) — the fall and rise of the tide, the changing level of the sea (to ebb = to fall, to go down; to flow = to rise, to come up)

kept a vigil (8), n.
— watched or waited for something or someone

Phrasal verbs and verb-preposition combinations

perked up (2) — became alert, attentive, awake

setting out for (4) — beginning a trip to, starting to go to

jutting out (8) — sticking out

Additional Vocabulary

Do you know these words and phrases?

____ hut (1)   ____ shore (7)

____ broken-hearted (1)   ____ to be swept off one's feet (7)

____ dimmer (5)   ____ amazement (10)

____ ashore (5)   ____ dismay (12)

____ lightning (7)   ____ to overwhelm (13)

____ towering (7)

Look them up or look for them in the workbook.

How Yogbo the Glutton Was Tricked

Benin

Once upon a time there lived a girl named Alougba. She was a hardworking little girl with keen bright eyes – a delight to her parents and relatives. No chore was too difficult for her. She never rested until her work was done. Alougba's favorite chore was to go to the forest to get firewood with other girls from neighboring villages. *(1)*

One day, she foolishly gathered too much firewood. She couldn't keep up with the others and was left behind. Darkness was descending upon the countryside. The load Alougba was carrying was heavy, the distance was long, and there was no one in sight. But Alougba didn't want to give up. She trudged on, through the sunset with the load on her head, her body drenched in sweat. *(2)*

To keep up her spirits, she sang to herself. Soon, her throat was dry, and she was desperate for a few swallows of cool water. Looking around, she caught sight of a large baobab tree with a hole in its trunk. "I hope there is water in the hole," Alougba thought, "for I am dying of thirst." *(3)*

Throwing her burden to the ground, she rushed toward the tree, and to her joy and great relief she found the hole filled with sparkling water. Alougba reached out and plunged her right hand into the hole to scoop up some of the cool water. But when she tried to withdraw her hand, it got stuck! She plunged her left hand into the hole to free her right hand, but it, too, got stuck! Helpless and handless, Alougba broke into tears and her cries floated away on the still evening air. *(4)*

It was then that Yogbo, a trickster well-known for gluttony, came from behind a clump of trees, grinning broadly. His trap had been successful. He gestured for Alougba to calm down. "Oh, what's the matter now, little girl?" he said in his oily voice. *(5)*

45

"Please help me," Alougba cried. "I was going to scoop up some water to drink, and now both my hands are stuck." *(6)*

Mumbling a few magic words, Yogbo pulled Alougba's hands free, but instead of letting her go, he brought a drum from behind the tree and forced her inside. For many days, while Alougba's parents and relatives and all the people in the village were looking for the missing girl, Yogbo went from one village to another, beating his drum. *(7)*

Whenever Yogbo reached a compound, he would beat his drum until people gathered around him, and he would ask, his voice full of excitement, "Do you want to hear a drum that sings like a human being?" *(8)*

And the people would say, "A drum that sings like a human being! Yes ... Let's hear it!" *(9)*

"Bring a lot of food and a lot of palm wine!" Yogbo the Glutton would reply, "for you cannot hear my singing drum unless you pay for it!" *(10)*

Once his demand was satisfied, Yogbo would set the drum on the ground in front of him and beat it for a brief moment, commanding: "Drum, my singing drum, sing a song." And the drum would break into song:

> "Adjai, my father, Seyi, my mother,
> I am inside Yogbo's drum.
> I sing at Yogbo's command.
> I am the one this song is coming from.
> Daybreak will not come,
> And yet the sun has risen.
> Nightfall hangs back,
> But the moon is on the horizon.
> I sing at Yogbo's command.
> I am the singer in the drum.
> It is your missing daughter
> This song is coming from." *(11)*

If Yogbo had had any common sense, he would never have let his captive sing that song, for she was singing for help, but Yogbo had no common sense. He only heard the call of hunger from his bottomless stomach, and wherever he went people marveled at Yogbo's singing drum. Children followed him everywhere. And wherever he went, he got a lot of money and plenty of food. That was what he demanded in payment for making his drum sing. And Yogbo would not touch his drum until he had received his payment. *(12)*

Word of Alougba's disappearance spread, however, and then one day, without knowing it, Yogbo came to Alougba's village. Alougba's parents had heard about Yogbo and their daughter's song. They prepared with great fore-thought. Cunningly, they extended a warm welcome to the trickster and cooked delicious dishes for him: roast beef seasoned with pepper, onion, garlic, and powdered shrimp; pounded cassava served with goatmeat sauce, and many other special dishes. They also provided plenty of palm wine. Yogbo licked his lips as his hosts laid out the food before him. *(13)*

As they had expected, Yogbo ate gluttonously. He ate as though starved since the day he was born. He ate and drank until his stomach ached. Then he belched and fell asleep. *(14)*

This was the moment Alougba's parents had been waiting for. While Yogbo was snoring and dreaming of mountains of food and rivers of palm wine, Adjai, Alougba's father, cut open Yogbo's drum and delivered his beloved daughter. Then he filled the drum with stones and patched it up. Seyi rejoiced at the recovery of her child. She gave her food and water and hid her in the bedroom. *(15)*

When Yogbo finally woke up, he took his drum and went on his way. He reached the next village and again demanded food and palm wine as the price for entertaining people with his singing drum, and his demand was satisfied. But when he laid his hands on the drum, commanding, "Drum, my singing drum, sing a song," there was a stony silence. Yogbo shook the drum desperately, for he knew he would have to say goodbye to the pleasures of gluttony unless he could make his drum sing. "Drum, my singing drum, sing a song," Yogbo commanded desperately. But what he got in answer was not a song, but the harsh sound of stones hitting stones. *(16)*

With the angry crowd at his heels, Yogbo fled in shame. And so it was that Yogbo the Glutton, a man of incomparable greed and cunning, finally met his match. *(17)*

How Yogbo the Glutton Was Tricked

Connecting to the story

Think about and discuss these questions:

What are the most famous foods in your country?

If you are not living in your country, what are some of the foods you miss most?

What foods do you recommend to visitors to your country? Describe them.

Glossary

(Numbers refer to the paragraph number)

Words

trudged (2), v. — walked slowly and tiredly with great effort

baobab tree (3), n.
— a large African tree with a very wide trunk and short branches

scoop (4), v.
— to pick up a handful of something in one motion

clump (5), n. — a group of plants growing together

mumbling (7), v. — speaking unclearly and too quietly

powdered (13), adj.
— dry, very small pieces of something; like dust

cassava (13), n. — a tropical vegetable similar to a potato

palm wine (13), n.
— an alcoholic drink made from palm nuts

belched (14), v. — let air out of the stomach through the mouth making a noise

Phrasal verbs and verb-preposition combinations

keep up with (2)
— maintain the same speed or level with others

give up (2) — discontinue, stop trying

patched up (15) — repaired

Additional Vocabulary

Do you know these words and phrases?

_____ glutton (title)   _____ helpless (4)

_____ chore (1)   _____ trap (5)

_____ foolishly (2)   _____ captive (12)

_____ drenched (2)   _____ marveled (12)

_____ desperate (3)   _____ cunningly (13)

_____ reached (4)   _____ harsh (16)

_____ plunged (4)   _____ fled (17)

Look them up or look for them in the workbook.

Monkey's Argument
With Leopard

Congo

Once upon a time Leopard woke from sleep and went forth from his den in search of food. The sun had just lifted its face above the horizon, flooding the heavens with light. The green grass glistened with dewdrops, and the forest was alive with birdsongs and the cries of a thousand creatures. Leopard lay in wait a long time, crouching on all fours, his ears perked up, ready to spring out for the kill, but neither antelope, nor buffalo, nor any other game wandered within range. *(1)*

As Leopard waited, a great, flaming anger came over him. "How long will I have to wait before I get something to eat!" he growled. "The way things are going, I might wait a whole day and have nothing to show for it!" And he went tearing through the forest, his sharp teeth shining like rows of knives held up to the sun. But then there was a great crash and Leopard was heard howling for help: "Help! Help! I have fallen into a well. Pull me out, some-body! Pull me out before I die. Pull me out, plea-ea-ea-ea-ea-se!" *(2)*

The well into which Leopard had plunged lay a short distance from a clump of trees where monkeys were at play. Some were hanging from the leafy branches by their feet, some were swinging from one tree to another, and some were racing each other to the top of the tallest trees and back. There was a general panic when the howls of the predator burst in upon their happy hour, and they vanished in a flash. *(3)*

They remained hidden from view a long time while the predator went on howling and pleading for someone to pull him out of the well. Then, realizing that they were in no

51

immediate danger, the monkeys came out of their hiding place and cautiously made their way toward the well, looking around carefully. But they all held back from getting too close. *(4)*

Finally, their leader, the tallest and strongest of them all, stepped boldly to the rim of the well and looked in. "The fellow is in trouble all right," he said, looking around at the other monkeys, a spiteful smile on his face. At this, they all rushed forward and soon the well was surrounded by a crowd of monkeys pushing for a good look at their enemy now at their mercy. From the bottom of the well, Leopard saw the monkeys looking down at him and pleaded as best he could:

> Pull me out, gentle monkeys! Please do not let me die.
> Save, save me now and we shall be friends for life.
> This is a solemn promise, which I will ever stand by.
> No longer will my kind and your kind be at strife! *(5)*

"No one will help you get out of that well," one monkey cried. "You have waged war on us since the days of our ancestors. You have never shown us any mercy. Why should we show you mercy now?" And the leader added:

> Plead until nightfall and you shall have pleaded in vain.
> There at the bottom of the well shall you ever remain.
> To me and my kind you have brought terror and death.
> We'll not be safe from danger so long as you have breath. *(6)*

The monkeys ignored the hunter's plea for help. Yet, Leopard went on begging for mercy, hoping beyond hope that they would pity him and save his life. He went on pleading until his voice grew faint. And when his voice had got so weak they could barely hear him, the monkeys drifted away, knowing that their enemy had but a little time left to live. *(7)*

But one of them could not quite bring himself to leave, for he was torn between hate and pity for the predator's cruel fate. Stooping over the rim of the well, he looked down at Leopard and spoke:

Do you really mean it, what I heard you say?
Never again will you seek and hunt us for your prey?
If we take pity, trust what you say, and save your life,
There will at last be peace between us, an end to all
strife? *(8)*

And the hunter replied with all the strength he could
muster:

As you and all the others have heard,
I have pledged my most solemn word.
If you should take pity and save my life,
There will be an end to enmity and strife. *(9)*

The monkey stepped back and went into the bush nearby.
It was not long before he came back holding a rope. "May
your word be your bond," he said as he lowered the rope
into the well. Quickly Leopard grabbed it and began his
climb while Monkey pulled and strained to keep his bal-
ance. Before long Leopard emerged from the well, but no
sooner had he touched ground than he grabbed his savior
by the tail, his eyes burning like fire, his claws sticking out
like the quills of a porcupine. *(10)*

"You are hurting me!" Monkey cried, trying to wriggle his
tail free from Leopard's grasp. *(11)*

"Hurting you!" Leopard growled. "I am going to eat you,
for I am very hungry." *(12)*

"How can you treat me so?" Monkey screamed. "Only a
moment ago you spoke words of peace and friendship. Let
me go, for you have given me your word!" *(13)*

But Leopard replied:

My words have as much substance as the breeze
Blowing among the tall and leafy trees.
Born and bred to love of blood and fresh meat,
I cannot let my word hinder my urge to eat. *(14)*

Monkey scolded Leopard for being such a cheat, de-
manding he let go of him at once. But Leopard was deter-
mined not to let go; it was his right as a hunter to catch
and eat monkeys! *(15)*

The two of them were still locked in a battle of words when Tortoise, who happened to be passing by, asked why they were arguing so loudly. *(16)*

"I really don't understand this at all!" Tortoise exclaimed after both Leopard and Monkey had told their side of the story. "Am I to believe that Monkey has enough strength in his arms to pull Leopard out of a well as deep as this?" he said, shaking his head in disbelief. "Tell me another joke.... I am not such a fool as I look." *(17)*

"But I did pull him out of the well, and my hands are still hurting," cried Monkey, holding his hands up for Tortoise to see. *(18)*

"You may argue as much as you want, but I won't believe either of you until I see with my own eyes this thing you claim to have done!" said Tortoise. *(19)*

"Let it never be said that I told a lie," Leopard growled, letting go of Monkey's tail. "Let's do it again so he can see the truth with his own eyes." *(20)*

So saying, Leopard jumped back into the well. Tortoise peered down after him to make sure Leopard had reached the bottom. Then he nodded several times and, turning around to face Monkey, waved goodbye to him and ambled off toward the setting sun. *(21)*

"Farewell," Monkey cried to Tortoise and went off in the opposite direction. *(22)*

At the bottom of the well, Leopard waited and waited for Monkey to pull him out so he could clear his name and eat his fill of monkey meat. Some say that Leopard is still waiting at the bottom of that well, wondering why Monkey has kept him waiting all these years. *(23)*

Monkey's Argument With Leopard

Connecting with the story

Think about and discuss these questions:

Have you ever been in a situation where a promise was broken? What was the result of breaking the promise?

Have you ever known about a situation where enemies helped each other? Explain.

Glossary

(Numbers refer to the paragraph number)

Words

den (1), n. — a place where animals live, usually a hole or cave

horizon (1), n. — the distant line between the sky and the earth

crouching (1), v. — bending the body to be close to the ground

vanished (3) v. – disappeard quickly

rim (5), n. — edge of something, frequently round

waged (6), v. — carried out, fought

wriggle (11), v. — move in short, quick motions

peered (21), v. — looked at closely

Phrasal verbs and verb-prepositions

spring out (1) — to jump suddenly from hiding

burst in upon (3) — suddenly interrupted, intruded on

Additional Vocabulary

Do you know these words and phrases?

____ to glisten (1)   ____ to ignore (7)

____ game (1)   ____ to drift (7)

____ flaming (2)   ____ fate (8)

____ to plunge (3)   ____ prey (8)

____ predator (3)   ____ strife (9)

____ to vanish (3)   ____ bond (10)

____ spiteful (5)   ____ emerged (10)

____ to rush (5)   ____ to hinder (14)

____ mercy (5)   ____ to amble (21)

Look them up or look for them in the workbook.

The Gold Ring

Benin

Once upon a time, there was a very powerful king. The king had seven sons. They were the most powerful princes in the world. They were tall, strong, and extremely intelligent. *(1)*

One day, the king brought them together and presented each one with a magnificent, finely-crafted gold ring, saying: "I will give each of you a ring. Each ring is unique. I give you the ring without asking for anything in return, except that each of you will bow down before me every morning and say, 'There is no power greater than the king, my father.' Each of you must guard his ring with his life. It is the supreme symbol of your loyalty to me, your father and your king. If you lose it, you will be executed." *(2)*

One by one six of the princes thanked the king for his marvelous gift. They praised him and promised to do everything he said. But the king's youngest son gave no promise. The king thought nothing of this. He was used to his youngest son's unpredictable character. He didn't think anyone could deny his power, especially not his quiet son. *(3)*

The next morning, there was a great celebration in praise of the king. The whole city could hear the beating of ceremonial drums and the singing of songs in praise of the king. Then, the seven princes arrived at the palace. *(4)*

The King was waiting in a room that had been especially prepared for the occasion. One by one, the seven princes came in. Each one bowed low before the king, saying, "There is no king on earth that is greater than the king, my father. I am his second in command." Each time a prince completed the ritual, the king smiled from ear to ear. *(5)*

When the youngest prince made his bow, however, the king became nervous. What was his unpredictable son going to say? After a long silence, the prince said, "The king, my father, is great. But the Creator is the greatest of all." The king was shocked. He frowned as he looked down at the youngest prince. Then, speaking in a calm, even voice, he expressed his deep appreciation for the love and respect of his wonderful sons and proclaimed that this ceremony would be a daily ritual. *(6)*

That same day, the king secretly sent for his youngest son's wife. "My dear daughter-in-law," he said, "I need your help with something extremely important." *(7)*

"What is it, my lord?" the prince's wife asked. *(8)*

"I want you to steal your husband's gold ring and bring it to me," the king said, "and I will pay you in silver and gold." *(9)*

"I can do it easily," the king's daughter-in-law answered, while her head filled with visions of silver and gold. *(10)*

That evening, the youngest prince's wife gave her husband a special dinner. She served him a selection of splendid dishes: yam with fish stew, black-eyed peas with palm oil, cassava flour, red corn paste with roast chicken. And of course she gave him plenty of palm wine to drink. After eating, he fell into a deep sleep. While he was sleeping, his wife removed the gold ring and took it to the king. The king rushed to the seaside and threw it into the sea. As he threw the ring away, he said, "Now I have a perfect excuse to teach my son a lesson." *(11)*

When the prince woke up in the morning, he discovered his ring was gone! He searched and searched, but it was nowhere to be found. His wife and all the servants helped him look for it. But the gold ring was not found. Everyone talked about the mysterious disappearance of the gold ring, including the prince's wife. *(12)*

Finally, the prince decided to tell the king about the missing ring. The king was furious! Shouting like thunder, his eyes shining with anger, he accused the prince of negligence and ingratitude: "Most unworthy, ungrateful son," he shouted, "I wish you were never born! You may never again call me your father! Yesterday you humiliated me and insulted me! Today you must pay the price. You put the Creator above me, but I am the most powerful of all kings! Unless the Creator can help you find the missing ring within seven days, you shall be executed!" After the king spoke, no one tried to speak in defense of the prince. Everyone feared the king when he was angry. *(13)*

Six days passed quickly, and soon the prince's execution was only one sunrise away. While awaiting death, the prince was kept under strict surveillance. He could not leave the city. But he could walk along the beach. He also had permission to eat whatever food he wanted during the final week of his life. On the sixth day, he suddenly felt a strong desire for one of his favorite dishes: broiled swordfish seasoned with salt, pepper, tomatoes, onion, and powdered shrimp. He decided this would be his last meal. *(14)*

The prince rose from the bed where he lay, paralyzed with fear and sadness. He walked to the beach. The sun was setting and all the fishermen had gone home. But then in the distance, he saw a man holding a big fish. The prince ran to the man, calling him and gesturing wildly. He thought delicious food was a special gift from the Creator. He had to eat his favorite dish once more before he was executed. *(15)*

The prince paid the man for the fish and took it home. When the prince got home and started to clean the fish, suddenly he saw a shining gold object in its mouth. When he looked closer, he saw it was the gold ring! He thought he was dreaming, so he rubbed his eyes and pinched himself. But the ring was still there. Then quick as a flash, he put the ring into his pocket and continued cleaning the fish. *(16)*

In the morning, at the time set for his execution, the prince was taken from his house to the public arena. The prince's six brothers and his father, the king, were waiting. The arena was full of people. Suddenly, the prince knelt down in front of the king. Then he took the gold ring from his pocket and held it high. "My father, the king is great and powerful," he said, "but the Creator is the greatest of all." The king was shocked, as he recognized the very same ring he had thrown into the sea a week before! The crowd filled the air with a thousand cries of wonder, relief, and delight. The king dropped to his knees and said over and over again, "Compared to the Creator, I am like a single grain of sand on a beach." *(17)*

In the great celebration that followed, the prince was proclaimed heir to the throne and chief advisor to the king. His wife was exposed as a thief and sent to jail. *(18)*

And so it was the belief grew among the people in that kingdom, in all the kingdoms of the region, that no king, however strong or powerful, could take the name of the Creator in vain. *(19)*

The Gold Ring

Connecting to the story

Think about and discuss these questions:

What was the best gift you ever received? Do you still have it? Explain what made it special.

What was the most important gift you ever gave to someone? What did it mean to you? What did it mean to the other person?

Glossary

(Numbers refer to the paragraph number)

Words

proclaimed (6), v. — announced, declared publicly and officially

negligence (13), n. — carelessness

ingratitude (13), n. — not grateful; not appreciating

surveillance (14), n. — careful observation of a person, usually a suspected criminal

heir to the throne (18), n. — the successor to the king or queen

Additional Vocabulary

Do you know these words and phrases?

_____ magnificent (2)   _____ ritual (6)

_____ unique (2)   _____ to humiliate (13)

_____ to bow (down) (2)   _____ to paralyze (15)

_____ to be executed (2)   _____ to gesture (15)

_____ to praise (3)   _____ throne (18)

_____ unpredictable (3)   _____ region (19)

_____ to deny (3)   _____ in vain (19)

_____ shocked (6)

Look them up or look for them in the workbook.

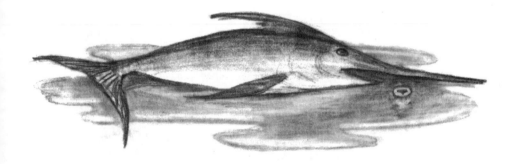

The Prince and the Orphan

Benin

My story flies over countries and kingdoms of long ago and alights on a prince. The prince was the king's only son. All of the children before him had died, one after another. Two months before the prince was born, the king consulted the royal diviner, and this was what he said:

> "A male child will be born to you.
> His name will be a secret to him,
> A secret to his mother,
> and a secret to all your subjects.
> Only in this way can he live.
> When he grows to be a man,
> Many women will desire his love,
> But only one can have it.
> She will be his partner.
> Only through their union
> Can he fulfill his destiny." *(1)*

When the baby was born, the king had a secret naming ceremony, with only his diviner present. The prince was named Denangan, which means "One of Them Shall Live." Never was a more handsome prince born to a king, and he grew more handsome as he grew into adulthood. He was tall and slender. His voice was deep. His eyes were bright, and he was always full of energy. His smile could bring happiness to a heart of stone. *(2)*

The king's subjects, however, loved him because of his kindness and the unusual wisdom which shone through his words and deeds. In addition, he was known throughout his father's kingdom as a champion of the poor and the powerless. *(3)*

67

When the prince grew to be a man, he began to feel the desire for a wife. The king decided that whoever could guess the prince's name would claim him for her husband. The good news of the king's decision spread throughout the kingdom. It excited the imaginations of a thousand young ladies. *(4)*

Among these, there was an orphan named Hobami, the poorest woman ever to fall in love with a prince. She was a tall, graceful girl with long, black hair, and big, brown eyes. Her stepmother, who had three daughters of her own, made Hobami work ceaselessly from early morning until late at night. *(5)*

Hobami's three stepsisters made no secret of their burning desire to marry the prince. They had definite plans for sweeping him off his feet. Their mother had ordered expensive clothes and jewelry so the sight of them would take the prince's breath away. And she planned to pay a diviner to reveal the prince's secret name. As the day of the contest drew near and their excitement reached fever-pitch, Hobami's stepsisters grew more and more boastful. *(6)*

"From the moment the prince looks at me, he will have eyes for no one else," said one. *(7)*

"My smile will cast such a powerful spell on the prince that he will beg me to marry him on the spot," said another. *(8)*

"When my turn to say the prince's name comes, my voice will sound so sweet in his ears that he will do anything to keep me by his side all the days of his life," the third sister said. *(9)*

The voices of Hobami's stepsisters rang in her ears as she started on one of her interminable errands. Pressing her hands to her breast, she cried, "I wish I too had a mother who could dress me up as a princess! Then my joy would know no bounds, for I would not be my stepsisters' laughingstock, but their equal. I would be worthy of the prince's love!" But Hobami had no one to give her a helping hand. *(10)*

On the day of the contest, Hobami's stepmother called her three daughters together and handed them the beautiful clothes and the priceless jewels she had bought especially for them. And while the three sisters were jumping up and down and screaming with joy, she called Hobami and gave her a bundle of rags, saying, "The king requires all the young women in the land to take part in the contest this evening. I wish you could dress up like everyone else, but this is all I could afford. You may go as soon as you complete your chores." *(11)*

And while Hobami was busy getting water, cleaning dishes, washing clothes, and sweeping the floor, her step-sisters washed themselves, rubbed their bodies with a fragrant ointment and put on their makeup. Then, wearing their splendid garments and jewels, they called Hobami so she could see how beautiful they looked. *(12)*

"It's a pity we have to leave while you are still doing your chores ... but we will put a palm branch at the crossroad so you will find your way to the palace without difficulty," they said. Then they set out for the king's palace and soon came to the crossroad. They knew that the path to the right led to the palace, but they put a palm branch across the path to the left and went on their way. *(13)*

At a bend in the path, they came upon an old woman, a spirit in disguise. "My children, give me something to eat, for I am starving," she pleaded, holding out her withered hands. *(14)*

"You witch!" one of the sisters snorted. "How dare you call me your daughter!" *(15)*

"My mother is far younger and much more beautiful than you, old hag!" another sister hissed. *(16)*

"You get out of our way before I pick you up and throw you into the bush!" the third sister roared. And the three sisters roughly pushed the old woman aside and moved on, laughing at their own remarks. *(17)*

The sun had vanished from the sky and darkness was slowly settling over the village when Hobami completed her final task. Quickly, she washed herself and put on the tattered clothes her stepmother had given her. Then she wrapped a few bean cakes in banana leaves to eat along the way and set out on the long journey to the king's palace. *(18)*

She soon came to the crossroad and stood looking, now to the left, now to the right, for the palm branch her sisters said they would put across the path leading to the palace. Suddenly a whirlwind arose and enveloped Hobami in a thick cloud of dust. When it finally blew away, the palm branch lay across the path to the right. So Hobami turned right and went on her way. *(19)*

Hobami had only gone a few yards when she came upon the same old woman her stepsisters had insulted and ridiculed. The old woman stood across Hobami's path, with her hands stretched out toward Hobami. "Give me something to eat, my child, for I am dying of hunger," she implored. *(20)*

"I do not have much, but the little I have I'll share with you," Hobami replied. She unwrapped the bean cakes she had brought with her and gave the old woman an equal share. "Now, if you will excuse me, I must be on my way, for I am late," Hobami said. *(21)*

"Where are you going so late at night?" the woman asked. *(22)*

"To the king's palace, to try my luck at guessing the handsome prince's name," Hobami replied. "But now that I think of it," she went on, "I haven't the foggiest idea what the prince's name is." *(23)*

"I know the prince's name," the old woman said, smiling gently and taking Hobami's hands in her own, "and since you have been so kind to me and given me food, I will tell you. Because all the king's children who were born before him had died in infancy, the king named the prince Denangan, which means 'One of Them Shall Live.'" *(24)*

Hobami thanked the woman over and over and begged her to say more about the prince, but she vanished, leaving Hobami dazed with curiosity. *(25)*

When Hobami reached the royal palace, the last contestant was walking away, her head hanging in shame, andshe joined the sorrowful multitude who had failed the name-guessing test. The sudden appearance of the ragged but pretty girl drew laughter and insults from all around. Hobami's three stepsisters were bitter about their own failure. They were angry that Hobami was trying to succeed where they had failed. They rushed forward and barred her way, their eyes blazing with anger, their hair standing on end. *(26)*

The king's diviner, who was in charge of the contest, sprang to his feet. He ordered the sisters back to their seats, and commanded the crowd to be quiet. Then, he motioned Hobami forward. "Do you know the name of the prince?" he asked her. *(27)*

"Denangan. That's his name," she said, her heart racing out of control. As she fell silent, there broke forth a roll of drums, and a thousand exclamations of wonder and amazement went soaring to the skies. The handsome prince came out from the secret chamber where he had been confined throughout the contest. He walked toward Hobami, his arms open wide, smiling radiantly. *(28)*

Ashamed of their lack of kindness and fearful of Hobami's revenge, the three stepsisters and their mother fled from one village to another. But Hobami wanted no revenge and left them to their own consciences. The cruelty of Hobami's step-family became the subject of numerous songs that followed the fugitives like a curse all the days of their lives. As for Hobami, she and her husband lived a long and happy life and had many children. *(29)*

The Prince and the Orphan

Connecting to the story

Think about and discuss these questions:

Are children's names important in your culture?

How was your name chosen?

How do you think children's names should be chosen?

Glossary

(Numbers refer to the paragraph number)

Words

diviner (1), n.
— a fortune teller, a person who can see the future

subjects (3), n. — the people who are governed by the king

boastful (6), adj. — speaking of oneself in a very proud way

laughingstock (10), n.
— the victim of jokes, a person whom others laugh at

dazed (25). adj. — dizzy; confused

Additional Vocabulary

Do you know these words and phrases?

_____ orphan (title)

_____ deeds (3)

_____ throughout (3)

_____ ceaselessly (5)

_____ fever-pitch (6)

_____ a spell (8)

_____ priceless (11)

_____ chores (11)

_____ garments (12)

_____ disguise (14)

_____ to starve (14)

_____ withered (14)

_____ to vanish (18)

_____ tattered (18)

_____ to implore (20)

_____ multitude (26)

_____ to bar (26)

_____ amazement (28)

_____ radiantly (28)

_____ ashamed (29)

_____ fugitive (29)

Look them up or look for them in the workbook.

Cultural Readers • Stories and Plays
also available from *Pro Lingua*

Story Cards. All ages, advanced beginners to advanced. The students get a card, study it, and then tell the story from memory to a partner or to the class. Excellent guided speaking practice that is also fun and informative. Three different sets are available:

- *North American Indian Tales.* 48 animal stories from tribes across the continent. Color illustrations of each story.

- *Aesop's Fables.* 48 classic fables known the world over. Color illustrations.

- *The Tales of Nasreddin Hodja.* 40 stories about the legendary Turkish humorist with an incomparable sense of humor and ageless common sense. Smiles, laughs, and wonderful illustrations.

Stranger in Town. High school to adult. Intermediate to advanced proficiency. A dramatic play in four acts for reading aloud or even for a class performance. 18 characters weave through the play as the stranger with a past arrives in town and takes up residence and responsibility. It's an allegory for the process of learning and cultural adjustment. *Cassette available.*

Celebrating American Heroes. All ages and proficiency levels. 13 brief plays about significant historical figures from Sacagawea to Cesar Chavez. They are designed for reading aloud dramatically. In each play there are a few main characters and a chorus that comments and advises by chanting about the actions of the heroes. Everybody participates. *Teacher's Guide* **(photocopyable)** and *Cassette available.*

Pro Lingua Associates
P. O. Box 1348, Brattleboro, VT 05302-1348

(800) 366-4775 • www.ProLinguaAssociates.com

The Origin of Cedar Trees
Haida

After the world was made, the Creator put the Haida
Indians on the land that is now called the Queen Char-
lotte Islands. "This is a good place. You will be happy
here," the Creator said. But soon the Haidas began to
quarrel and fight. The Creator came back to the Haidas
and said, "If you cannot live together in peace, I will
punish you." The Haidas promised they would live
happily ever after, but it did not take long before they
were arguing again.

The Creator came again and told the Haidas, "You
knew I would punish you if you could not live in peace."
Instantly He changed all the people into cedar trees.
"Now when people come to these islands, they will see
you and remember what happens when you cannot live
in peace."

But from evil comes good. The Haidas who came later
to the islands used the cedar trees to build houses and
canoes. From the roots they made baskets and mats, and
from the bark fibers they wove clothing.   23 (S:6)

A sample of **North American Indian Tales.** © 1995 Susannah J. Clark

The Rabbits and the Frogs

Once upon a time the rabbits had a meeting. They were very tired of being afraid. They were tired of running away from all the other animals. They decided to do something. One rabbit suggested that life was not worth living. "Let's all go to the lake. We will jump in together and drown ourselves. Then our troubles will be over."

So they ran toward the lake. Just as they reached the shore, all the frogs on the shoreline jumped into the water because of the noise made by the rabbits. One of the older rabbits turned to its friends and said, "Let's think about this some more, my friends, because it seems the frogs are afraid of us."

#17

A sample of **Aesop's Fables.** © 1995 Raymond C. Clark

One day Hodja came back from the market with a very nice piece of meat for dinner. He left it with his wife and went out to have a cup of tea.

While he was gone, his wife prepared a wonderful shish kebab, but it looked and smelled so good she couldn't resist tasting it. Just then some of her friends came by, and in a short time the meat was all gone.

Hodja returned for dinner, but his wife served him a thin, watery soup instead of the meat.

"But where is the meat?" asked Hodja.

"Oh, the cat ate it," said his wife.

"But it was a whole kilo," said Hodja. He then found the cat and put it on the scales. It weighed one kilo.

"So, I have found the meat," Hodja said, "Now, where is the cat?"

31